Coaching Ms. Parker

Coaching Ms. Parker

by Carla Heymsfeld
illustrated by Jane O'Conor

First Aladdin Paperbacks edition 1995
Text copyright © 1992 by Carla Heymsfeld
Illustrations copyright © 1992 by Jane O'Conor
Aladdin Paperbacks
An imprint of Simon & Schuster
Children's Publishing Division
1230 Avenue of the Americas
New York, NY 10020

The text of this book is set in 14-point Sabon.
Printed in the United States of America
10 9 8 7 6 5 4 3 2
The Library of Congress has cataloged the hardcover edition
as follows:
Heymsfeld, Carla.
Coaching Ms. Parker / by Carla Heymsfeld : illustrated by Jane
O'Conor. — 1st ed.
p.   cm.
Summary: Mike and his friends try to help their fourth-grade
teacher learn how to play baseball before the annual
teacher-student game.
ISBN 0-02-743715-9
[1. Baseball—Fiction.   2. Schools—Fiction.   3. Teacher-student
relationships—Fiction.]   I. O'Conor, Jane ill.   II. Title.
PZ7.H475Co   1992
[Fic]—dc20   91-28484

ISBN 0-689-71830-6

For David, Ralph, and David Jr.,
who were patient and supportive;
for the Tuesday Nighters,
who listened and advised;
for the teachers at Westbriar,
who played the game;
and for Mr. C.,
who made them do so.

Contents

1 The Announcement • 1
2 The Plan • 12
3 Problems • 22
4 Two-Way Street • 33
5 The Coach • 42
6 Surprises • 50
7 Practice, Practice, Practice • 63
8 The Game • 75

Coaching Ms. Parker

1
ooo
The Announcement

"You ready?" A familiar face peeked in the kitchen door. Mike's best friend, Ho-Pu, was here. Every day he came by to walk with Mike to school.

"I'm coming," Mike said, grabbing his baseball glove and mask. "Don't call me from work this afternoon," he told his mother. "I'll be late. We're playing ball after school."

"So what else is new?" Mrs. Fisher waved hello to Ho-Pu, who waved his glove back.

"I'll start worrying when you guys tell me you're *not* playing ball."

Mike grinned. Everyone knew it: there was nothing he'd rather do than play baseball. He scooped his lunch money into his pocket, stuck his cheek in the air for his mother's kiss, and followed Ho-Pu out the door.

"Let's see your glove," Mike said.

Ho-Pu passed it over.

"Did you put linseed oil on it like I said?"

Ho-Pu nodded.

Mike tested it by punching his right hand into the center of the mitt. "It's coming along fine. Soon the ball will fall in there all by itself."

"I don't think so. I don't catch as well as you."

"Sure you do," Mike said generously. "You just have to practice." Secretly, however, he thought Ho-Pu was right. He *could* catch better than his friend. In fact, he was the best fielder on his fourth grade team and one of the best in Little League.

Ho-Pu reclaimed his glove and shoved it into his book bag. Then, rooting around the bottom of the canvas sack, he pulled out a notebook. "Are you ready to turn in your journal?" he asked.

Mike's stomach lurched. "Not exactly," he said. The truth was, Mike had eight blank days in his journal. He'd forgotten that Ms. Parker was going to collect them today. He wondered if he could write eight days of reading responses in the ten minutes between the first and second bell. It was not a happy thought.

Ho-Pu gave him a sympathetic look. "Why didn't you do your journal?" he asked. "It's not so hard. All you have to do is write down ideas you have about the book you're reading."

Mike tried to think of a book he could write about. Maybe something the librarian had read to the class.

Ho-Pu stopped walking and turned to him.

"Haven't you been reading?" he asked.

"Well, not that much." Mike looked away. Even though he could read pretty well, Mike didn't like books. No, that wasn't right. He didn't dislike books. It was just that there were so many things he liked better. Baseball, for example. Or soccer or basketball or computer games. Hiking with his father. Riding his skateboard. He couldn't seem to make time in his life for books.

"Look," Ho-Pu offered, "I'll tell you about the book I read last week and you can write about it, too."

Mike was flooded with gratitude. For the rest of the walk to school, he listened to Ho-Pu read from his notebook and tell as much as he could remember about *How to Eat Fried Worms*. It sounded like a good book. He was almost sorry he hadn't read it.

By the time the second bell rang, Mike's fingers were stiff and his hand was cramping.

But he didn't care. The important thing was, the panic was over and his stomach was feeling better. As soon as he'd come into class, he'd pulled out his journal and started writing. He wrote down everything he could remember that Ho-Pu had told him about *How to Eat Fried Worms*. It turned out to be quite a lot.

As Ms. Parker walked around the room collecting their notebooks, Mike turned his attention to his favorite part of the day, recess. The clock above the doorway moved slowly toward 10:30. Every few minutes, Mike felt for his glove in his desk. Most of the other kids put theirs in the coat closet. Mike never did. He wasn't worried about anyone stealing his—though that's what he told Ho-Pu—he simply liked having it near him.

He had just touched the smooth leather for the twenty-third time that morning when the classroom door opened. Mike sat up straighter when he saw Angel Velez come in, carrying a large poster. Angel was the biggest and the

best athlete in the sixth grade. Good enough to play soccer with the thirteen-and-over league, he was also a star on the baseball diamond. Mike's sister, Laura, who was in Angel's class, said that Mr. Curtis, the high school baseball coach, was already watching Angel pitch.

Angel propped his poster on Ms. Parker's desk. "Hear ye! Hear ye!" he cried, as if he were a king's messenger.

Now everyone else sat up and paid attention. Even Ms. Parker. "Two weeks from tomorrow," Angel boomed, "will be the Annual Baseball Game between the sixth graders and the teachers of Westbend Elementary. We will play on the field in back of the school at exactly 2 o'clock. All classes are invited."

Everybody cheered. Angel looked pleased. "I hope you guys will root for us," he added.

Everybody cheered again. Except for the little kids in kindergarten and a few of the first and second graders, the students of Westbend

Elementary always supported the sixth grade team. Mike hoped that this year his sister wouldn't embarrass him too much.

A hand tapped at Mike's right shoulder. He turned. There was Kathy, grinning at him and tugging her left braid the way she did when she got excited. He knew how she felt. Making a circle with his thumb and forefinger, Mike grinned back. The game between the sixth graders and the teachers was the most exciting school event all year.

Encouraged by the fourth graders' enthusiasm, Angel continued. "We have a really tough team this year," he said, his voice growing louder, "and we're gonna cream them." He threw his fist into the air like the guys did in the big leagues. Then, turning to Ms. Parker, he asked, "What position do *you* play?"

"None," she said, smiling. "I'll just be the cheering section."

"You can't do that," Angel said. "You have to play. It's tradition."

"Yeah!" a voice called out. "All the teachers play." It was Frank, class grump, whose gloomy point of view was usually just ignored. Today, however, he spoke for the class. Ms. Parker had no choice. She was a teacher at Westbend, and that meant she played baseball.

"But there are eleven teachers in the school," Ms. Parker insisted. "You only need nine players."

"Mrs. Peterson's got a bad ankle, and Miss Cole is too old." Angel looked down at Ms. Parker's ankles. "You don't have any problems, do you?"

Reluctantly, Ms. Parker shook her head.

"Then, that's that." Angel sounded relieved.

But Ms. Parker was not quite ready to give in. "If all the teachers are playing," she asked, "what happens to the students? Who takes care of them?"

"The room mothers come, like with class parties," Elizabeth explained. "Other parents come too, if they can. It's a pretty exciting game." Around the room, heads nodded in agreement.

As she listened, Ms. Parker stopped smiling. Her forehead wrinkled into a deep frown, and her mouth pinched into a tight line.

Gradually, the class quieted. Angel shuffled his feet. "Er, um," he said. "Yeah. It's gonna be great." But he didn't sound so sure anymore. He looked at Ms. Parker's unhappy face and backed out of the room. Without his support, the poster toppled to the floor.

The class sat in silence.

"You mad with us?" Yussif Assad finally asked. His words, spoken in Arabic-accented English, carried clearly to every part of the room.

Everyone waited for Ms. Parker's answer.

"No, Yussif," she said finally, "I'm just upset. I didn't know when I came here in September that I'd have to play baseball in May."

"You don't have to be good." Kathy tried to comfort her. "It's just for fun."

Ms. Parker was not convinced. "Baseball's not my sport at all," she said, picking up Angel's poster and propping it backward against the wall. "I'll be humiliated in front of the whole school."

How silly, Mike thought. Ms. Parker could jump rope faster and longer than anyone in the class except Gail Weinberg. And she could swim. Only last week, Kathy had told everyone how she'd seen her dive in and swim two laps at the Community Center pool. Ms. Parker probably just didn't know what she could do on a baseball field. The game wasn't all *that* hard to play.

2

The Plan

"How Ms. Parker not know baseball?" Yussif asked, as the class team gathered for their usual recess game. "Baseball is easy."

"I know." Mike gave his arm a friendly punch. "Especially for you. You're a good athlete."

Yussif smiled at the compliment. In September he'd known neither English nor baseball, but he'd learned both fast. Now he was everyone's first choice for second baseman, and thanks to Ms. Parker's help, his English got better every day. "Ms. Parker can not be so bad athlete," he said. "She knows everything."

"Particularly words," Elizabeth agreed. "She's a walking dictionary. I bet she can even spell 'antidisestablishmentarianism.' "

Elizabeth was pretty good with words herself. Mike wasn't sure he could even say such a long word, let alone spell it. Elizabeth was his friend because she could play baseball, but sometimes she annoyed him. She talked too much. And she was pushy, always trying to make everyone do things her way. Like now, she was pointing Ho-Pu in the direction of first base and shoving a bat in Gail's hand. It pleased Mike that Ho-Pu ignored her.

"I bet Ms. Parker would be able to play if she practiced a little," Ho-Pu said thoughtfully. "She probably just hasn't played since she was a kid."

Mike slipped the catcher's mask over his face, exchanged his glove for the class catcher's mitt, and nodded at his friend. "That's what I was thinking," he said. He looked across the playground, where Ms. Parker was watching some of the kids do perilous things on the gym set. "Why don't we ask her to work out with us after school? Once she hits a few balls and catches a little, she'll feel easier about the game."

"Suppose she really *is* bad at it?" Frank asked.

Voice of doom, Mike thought. When would the guy stop looking for trouble? Mike shrugged and looked away. Maybe, if no one encouraged him, Frank would drop the subject and fall in with the others.

Unfortunately, Yussif made a big point of rolling his eyes, and everybody laughed. The laughter made Frank more insistent. "What's so funny?" he complained. "If she says she can't play, she probably can't. She ought to know what she can do."

"C'mon, Frank," Mike said. "How bad can

she be? If last year's game says anything, most of the teachers aren't exactly ready for the majors. She'll fit in."

"Suppose she doesn't?" Frank would not let go.

"Well, then maybe Mike could teach her," Elizabeth suggested, snapping her thumb in Mike's direction. "He's our best player."

Mike stood a little straighter. Elizabeth might be a bit bossy, but at least she wasn't stupid. He smiled at her.

"What's going on here?" Kathy demanded, trying to tie her sneakers and walk at the same time. "Why aren't you playing ball?"

"We're going to get Ms. Parker in shape for the game—practice with her and stuff," Ho-Pu explained.

"Good idea!" Kathy nodded vigorously. "A little confidence and she'll be fine." Kathy was big on confidence. She'd turned herself into a steady, if unremarkable, pitcher by working hard and believing she could do it. "When do we start?" she asked.

The group shifted uneasily. "We haven't asked her yet," Ho-Pu admitted, "but I was thinking we'd start today after school."

"I can't stay after school," said Richie.

"Me neither." Penny shook her head. "I have to practice the piano."

"That's okay." Elizabeth dismissed Richie and Penny with a little wave. "We don't need *every*one."

"Well, we do need Ms. Parker. Who's going to ask her?" Mike looked around the group.

"She probably won't want to do it," Frank muttered.

Elizabeth glared at him. "Sure she will. Ms. Parker likes group projects."

"Yes," Frank glared back at her. "But she's never *been* a group project."

That stopped them. There was a long silence as they stared at one another.

"Well, who wants to tell her about it?" Mike asked again.

Everyone looked at him. Nobody volunteered. "You tell her," Ho-Pu said finally.

"Tell her what? What do I say?" Mike's enthusiasm was beginning to fade.

"Tell her we help. Say we teach her after school," Yussif offered. "Just for fun."

"Okay," Mike said. But it wasn't okay. What would Ms. Parker say when he raised the subject of baseball again? Mike felt sick. He felt even sicker as the group trudged across the playground and formed a little circle around their teacher.

"Is something wrong?" Ms. Parker asked. Several seconds passed. Mike swallowed hard. He couldn't seem to get started. Elizabeth gave him a little shove. "Mike has something to tell you," she said to Ms. Parker.

Mike wondered why Elizabeth, if she was so eager, didn't tell Ms. Parker herself. He looked at Elizabeth, who looked right back at him. It was like being trapped in a rundown. He took a deep breath. "Ms. Parker," he said, "we were wondering . . ." His voice trailed off helplessly. What *were* they wondering? Mike wished he could remember Yussif's words.

"Yes?" Ms. Parker lifted her eyebrows.

"We wondered . . . uh . . . if you'd like to come out after school and . . . er . . . play baseball with us. You know, practice a little for the . . . uh . . . game." There. He'd said it. He held his breath.

Ms. Parker nodded just a little. "That's very nice of you, Mike," she said kindly. "I understand what you are trying to do. But it won't work."

"Mike's a good teacher," Ho-Pu chimed in loyally.

Ms. Parker stared glumly at Mike. She did not seem convinced.

"All you need is a little practice," Kathy assured her.

"Wouldn't you help us if we couldn't do something?" Elizabeth demanded.

"Yeees," Ms. Parker dragged the word out.

Clearly, she was not an eager student. "I guess if you are willing to teach me, I ought to try to learn."

"Can you start this afternoon?" It was Elizabeth again. At least, Mike thought, she's persistent.

"I don't know. I don't have any sneakers with me." Ms. Parker looked down at her white suede sandals. "And don't you need to let your parents know if you are going to stay after school?"

"We could start tomorrow," Frank suggested. It was amazing what a little team spirit could do.

"I . . . I suppose that will be okay." Ms. Parker hesitated.

"Great!" Yussif cried. Then, before she could change her mind, they all ran back to the baseball diamond for the few minutes left of recess.

Mike grinned as he crouched down behind

home plate. Teaching the teacher. What a neat idea. His mind sorted through the tips his Little League coach had given them this year. He would pass them along.

Suddenly, Mike was jolted by the memory of Angel standing in front of the class. What would Angel think if he knew they were going to help Ms. Parker? And what about Laura? Would his sister think he was being a traitor? Mike shifted uneasily. Maybe Angel and Laura didn't have to know. Maybe he could teach Ms. Parker and still be loyal to the sixth grade.

Maybe.

3
ᵒᵒᵒ
Problems

Tuesday after school, Ms. Parker was greeted by a half-dozen coaches at the ball field. "Do you know the way the game is played?" Mike asked her. He had been rehearsing how to sum up the game and was having a hard time. "I mean the rules and stuff?"

Ms. Parker's head bobbed twice. "Sort of. I watch it on TV sometimes, and I've been to a few games."

"Good." The lesson was starting well.

Mike picked up his catcher's mask and took his place behind home plate. Ho-Pu ran out to first base, and Yussif took second. Frank, moving gracefully on his long legs, loped out to third.

"You're probably better than you think." Elizabeth stopped to encourage her teacher before going to the outfield. "Take the bat and try to hit Kathy's pitches. She'll send them over slow and easy."

Ms. Parker stood awkwardly at the plate, her feet close together, her hips pushed back, and her head cocked away from the bat. When Kathy's first pitch went over the plate nice and easy as promised, Ms. Parker scooped the bat like a croquet mallet. When the second pitch came in a little high, she swung as if she were chopping the ball with an ax.

"Swing like this," Frank called from third base. He wrapped his hands around an imaginary bat, pulled them back above his right shoulder, and swung.

Ms. Parker nodded and arranged her bat.

"Put it here, Ms. Parker," Elizabeth shouted, punching her fist into her mitt.

Ms. Parker tried to imitate Frank and at the same time aim for the outfield. Instead, she almost hit Mike in the head. "Oh, Mike," she said, "I am *so* sorry."

"Hey, that's all right," he assured her, but her batting made him nervous. "Why don't you do something easier, like throw?" He handed her the ball. "Toss it to Ho-Pu."

Ms. Parker threw it underhand. It went nearly thirty feet—straight up. Yelling, "Heads up," Mike positioned himself on home plate and caught the ball. "Try it overhand," he suggested, and showed her how to do it.

Ms. Parker's overhand landed in the dirt, about three feet away.

While Kathy coached Ms. Parker to try again, Elizabeth ran in from left field. Mike pulled off his catcher's mask and met her part way. "I'm coming in," Elizabeth whispered. "There's no point in standing out there. She's not going to get anything near me today."

"I know," Mike agreed. He watched his student aim the ball at first base. It went toward second.

"Do you think we can teach her in time for the game?" Elizabeth asked the dreaded question. "We only have two weeks."

Mike dug around in his mind for inspiring words. "If all we have is two weeks, then that's what we have," he said. It sounded like something his mom had said to him once. "We just have to take it one step at a time."

By the time Mike got home, dinner was on the table. "Where have you been?" his mother asked. "I've been worried sick. I called Ho-Pu's mother and Frank's mother. No one knew anything."

"I told you I'd be late."

"Not like this." His father scowled. "When

you're going to be this late, I want you to call."

"I'm sorry. We were playing ball. I didn't watch the time." Mike slid into his place.

"*Baseball*!" his mother said. "*Baseball, baseball, baseball.*" She rolled her eyes upward.

Laura, her mouth full of potatoes, chimed in. "You don't need to wear a baseball hat at the table, either."

"Don't talk with your mouth full," Mike reminded her. "You're spitting all over the place." He grinned when he saw her face turn red. Lately, Laura was an even bigger pain than she used to be. Any time she wasn't looking in the mirror or talking on the telephone, she was telling him how to behave. It felt good to catch her doing something wrong.

Laura sniffed loudly. "I bet you never even washed up before you sat down," she said. "You smell."

Mike wondered if it were true. He was

pretty sure she was too far away to know. "What you're smelling are your feet," he said. "Put your shoes back on."

"My shoes *are* on. Dad, how can you let him . . ."

"Let's stop this," Mrs. Fisher cut her off. "I don't want any more fighting at the table."

"Yeah," Mike said, looking innocent. "Let's not fight." Now that he'd gotten her ruffled by being nasty, he figured he could make her madder by being nice.

And he was right. "Mom," Laura wailed. "He's just trying to . . ."

"Laura was telling us about the game," Mr. Fisher interrupted the melee. "She says the sixth grade is going to win. What do you think?"

Mike thought about Ms. Parker. She was the sixth grade's secret weapon, even if they didn't know it. Unless she improved tremendously in the next two weeks, her bumbling at bat and in the field would make the sixth grade victory easier than usual. Of course, he couldn't say these things now. Not in front of Laura. His sister would blab to everyone. Besides, it might be too early to tell. Maybe Ms. Parker had some hidden talents that would emerge after she got going. Mike kept his expression bland as he shrugged and said, "The sixth grade usually wins. They'll probably win this year, too. Depends on the team, I guess."

"We've got a great team," Laura boasted. She looked smug.

"With you on it?"

"Why shouldn't I be good?" Laura scowled.

"Because you don't play baseball. What are you going to hit the ball with? Your tennis racket?"

"Tennis players make good ballplayers," Mr. Fisher said. "They already have their eyes and hands working together."

"You need more than eyes and hands to play baseball," Mike complained.

"Like what?" Laura snapped. "A big mouth?"

Mr. Fisher shot Laura a warning look. Then he pointed his fork in Mike's direction. "Why don't you practice with your sister?" he suggested. "Take her out after school. Help her with her hitting and fielding. She can use the old mitt your cousin Peter left here last summer."

"Good night!" Laura threw herself back in her chair and looked at the ceiling.

"What's the matter, Laura?" Mr. Fisher asked. "It's a great idea. I've watched Mike coach Ho-Pu and Yussif. He's a fine teacher."

Mike chewed his lip. How could he stay after school to teach Ms. Parker and coach his sister, too? "If I practice with Laura after school, I can't play with the guys," he moaned. His father liked him to play with his friends.

"Nonsense." Mr. Fisher didn't buy Mike's excuse. "You can do both. Just come home a little earlier. You can work with your sister in the backyard before dinner."

"He doesn't have to if he doesn't want to," Laura said, looking at Mike suspiciously.

"Of course he wants to," Mrs. Fisher assured her. "He's your brother. We help each other in this family."

"Yeah," Mike said, cornered. He tried to look sincere. "I'll help you. You don't want to look like a jerk in the game." He could tell his parents were pleased. He even thought he saw a flicker of gratitude on Laura's face. He looked away. What would Laura think if she knew he was also coaching the opposition?

Later, Laura knocked on Mike's door. He was sitting in the middle of his bed rubbing linseed oil into his glove. She watched him for a minute before she spoke. "What are you doing?"

"The oil softens the mitt," he explained.

"Softens?"

"So I can shape it. After I oil it, I put a ball

in it. Then I wrap the glove with a rubber band. After a while, the glove has a nice round pocket. Helps the ball stay in."

"Oh." Laura watched a little longer. "Can I have some oil for Peter's old glove?" she asked.

"Sure," he said, waiting. He knew this was not the reason for her visit.

"I appreciate your helping me," she said finally.

"That's okay." Mike didn't look up. "Dad's probably right. You'll catch on fast."

"And Mike . . ." She hesitated. "I'm sorry I said you smelled. You didn't. I just said it because I was mad."

"I know." This time Mike did look up. "It's okay," he said again.

He just hoped she'd show more promise than Ms. Parker.

4
°°°
Two-Way Street

The next morning, Mike reached under his mattress and gently pulled his mitt from its night's rest. He took off the rubber band and let the ball roll out of the plastic bag. He was pleased with what he saw. The pocket was looking better and better.

Mike never used a regular ball for this job. He always used the one that his grandfather had given him for his seventh birthday. Reverently, he pulled it from the protective bag and studied the faded black letters that made it so special: M-I-C-K-E-Y M-A-N-T-L-E. Mike could still remember the look on Grandpa's face when he explained how he'd caught it in the stands at Yankee Stadium and went to the dugout to get it signed.

Although Mike did not generally believe in magic, he had a feeling about this ball. A ball that had once been whacked by a home-run slugger like Mickey Mantle might have a little luck in it. Certainly, letting it sit in his glove couldn't hurt. He lifted it close to his nose and breathed deeply. Then he slid it into his night table drawer and got ready for school.

Mike spent the morning planning his second coaching session. He thought about it as he listened to morning announcements. He thought about it all through math. By the time he finished his spelling test, he'd decided that the first thing to do was to get Ms. Parker to stand right.

He was so involved in his plans, it seemed perfect timing when Ms. Parker called him to the back of the room. He smiled at her as he sat in one of the chairs at the round conference table.

"We have a little problem, Mike," she said.

He almost told her not to worry. He almost said, "It's no problem. You'll be fine once we get started." Luckily, she spoke first.

"I read your journal last night," she said.

"Oh." His mouth was suddenly dry.

"When I read it, I wondered if you'd ever read *How to Eat Fried Worms*."

Mike ran his tongue over his upper lip. "What do you mean?" he asked.

She looked at him for several long seconds. "You know what I mean," she said.

Mike could not meet her eyes. He studied a jagged mark on the table that someone had carved with a pencil.

"Mike?" Ms. Parker prodded gently.

Still not meeting her eyes, he shook his head.

"Why did you do it? You're a good enough reader."

Mike kept staring at the hole in the table. How could she tell he hadn't read it? He'd written down everything Ho-Pu told him.

"Mike." Ms. Parker's voice became sharper. "Look at me."

Mike forced his eyes up.

"When you turn in a response for a book you didn't read, you're telling a lie."

Her words felt like a slap in the face. "I didn't have anything else to write," he said. "I just wanted to have something to turn in."

"Why not write about a book you read yourself?"

"I didn't have one." His voice cracked a little. Once again Mike looked down. He waited for her to ask why he didn't have a book, but she didn't. Instead, Ms. Parker got up and walked across the room.

Mike watched her as she looked in a box of books. She pulled out two. One was fat and the other was real skinny. If they're for me, I'll pick the skinny one, Mike decided. Ms. Parker didn't come back, however. She went to another box. This time she pulled three books out. She looked around the room. Suddenly, she snapped her fingers and walked to the bookcase. She bent over and looked on the bottom shelf. When she found what she wanted, she turned and came back to Mike.

"Sometimes it's hard to find a good book," she said. "So I picked out some I think you might like." She dumped her pile on the table. "Here are a couple about sports." She pushed the fat one and the skinny one from the first box in front of Mike. "And here are some funny ones. *The Chocolate Touch* is good. So is *Tales of a Fourth Grade Nothing.* If you haven't read *The 18th Emergency*, you might try it. It's about a boy who writes the name of the class bully next to a picture of a caveman, and the bully catches him doing it."

"That doesn't sound so funny." Mike could

imagine himself getting caught like that and didn't like the feeling.

Ms. Parker laughed. "I guess I didn't describe it very well. Betsy Byars is a wonderful writer, and she really did make it into a great story." The last book, the one Ms. Parker had picked out of the bookcase, she kept close to her. "This is one of my favorites," she said. "It's more serious, but it is very interesting. It's about a strange man who traveled around Connecticut and New York over a hundred years ago."

Mike peeked at the title, *The Leatherman*. The cover had a huge, ghostly man walking behind a boy about Mike's age. Mike reached for it.

"You don't have to choose one now, Mike," Ms. Parker said. "Take any you think you might like to your seat. Look through them. Maybe one will turn out to be right for you."

Mike picked up the skinny sports book and *The Chocolate Touch*. He also took *The*

Leatherman. Something about the book tugged at him. "Thanks," he said.

"Look at this one, too." Ms. Parker pushed the fat sports book across the table. "I think it has a chapter on the history of baseball."

"It looks like the history of the world." Mike let the book sit where she'd left it.

Ms. Parker laughed. "I know. It's a big book. But don't let that scare you off. You don't have to read everything in it. Just find the parts that interest you."

That's what kids did, Mike knew. He didn't realize that it was allowed. He pulled the book into his pile.

"Choosing books and writing in your journal is hard for you, isn't it?" Ms. Parker asked.

Mike nodded.

"I know. We all find something hard. For me, it's baseball."

"You'll be okay," Mike said.

"So will you," his teacher answered. "I'll work on baseball. You work on reading and writing about your books in your journal. Okay?"

"Yeah." Mike grinned.

"And telling the truth," Ms. Parker added. "I want to know I can believe in you."

Mike stopped grinning. "You can. I promise." His voice was low, but he looked right at her so she'd know he meant it.

She nodded solemnly. "Good." Then, leaning forward, she confided, "That's what I like about this school. It's a two-way street. We trust and help each other here."

5
The Coach

That afternoon Mike and the others took Ms. Parker out to practice. "First you have to learn how to stand," Mike told her. He picked up a bat and arranged himself in the correct position. "See my feet? I've got them spread apart, about as wide as my shoulders. And my knees—see how they're bent?"

Ms. Parker nodded and spread her feet and bent her knees.

"Good," Mike said. "Now lean forward

and put your weight on the balls of your feet."
He showed her what he meant.

Ms. Parker stood on her toes and began to
wobble.

"No. No. Not that much!" Kathy reached
out to steady her. "Your heels still have to
touch the ground."

Ms. Parker settled back down.

"That's right," Mike said, smiling in en-
couragement. "Now take the bat."

Ms. Parker grabbed the bat and plopped it
on her shoulder. It hung down her back like
a dead snake.

Mike shook his head. "Not like that. Pick
it up off your shoulder and hold it with your
fingers. You've got it way back in your palms."

Ms. Parker looked at him as though he had
just spoken in another language.

Ho-Pu reached over and moved the bat forward in her hands. "Here's what Mike
means," he said.

"It feels weird," Ms. Parker complained.

"I'll drop it if I hold it like this."

"You're just not used to it." Mike watched the bat bobble around and wondered if she *was* going to drop it. He grabbed the end and held it until she got it under control. "Try to swing now," he said.

Ms. Parker swung the bat. It would have been a good swing for beating a rug on a clothesline. It was not good for baseball.

"As you swing, you turn your body and your shoulders move," Frank explained. He picked up a bat and showed her how to do it.

Ms. Parker nodded her understanding and tried a swing.

"Not bad," Yussif said. "Just follow through a little more."

"Like this?" asked Ms. Parker. Suddenly the bat was flying through the air.

"Watch out," Ho-Pu yelled. Everybody ducked.

"You've got to be more careful," Mike said. Fear made his voice stern. "Whatever you do, hold on to your bat."

Ms. Parker's eyes were huge. "I'm sorry, Mike," she whispered.

Mike sighed. "Try again," he said.

Ms. Parker tried a few more swings.

"You're getting it," Mike told her. "You're doing well now."

His teacher grinned.

"I think you're ready to try hitting a ball." Mike tossed a ball to Kathy, who ran out to the pitcher's mound. Ho-Pu ran toward first base, and Elizabeth, taking over Mike's spot, put on the catcher's mask and crouched behind home plate.

Kathy threw the ball.

By the time Ms. Parker swung, Elizabeth had already caught it.

Kathy threw the ball again.

This time Ms. Parker swung too early.

Mike decided to help. The next time Kathy pitched, he yelled "*now*" when it was time to swing.

Startled, Ms. Parker jumped and dropped the bat. "Gosh, Mike. I didn't expect that."

Mike shook his head. "Hold on to the bat. You've *got* to hold on." He could feel his patience leaking away.

"Try stepping forward when you swing," Frank suggested. "It gets you started right."

When the next pitch came in, Ms. Parker stepped forward, but she forgot to swing. The next time, she remembered to swing but forgot to step forward. "I'll never get this," she said, her shoulders drooping.

"You'll be fine," Mike said. "It takes time."

Ms. Parker looked doubtful.

"Yes, yes. Mike is correct," Yussif assured her. "You look much more good today. Tomorrow you will hit a ball."

Mike hoped Yussif was right. She sure wasn't going to hit one today. He studied his teacher's bleary eyes, the smears of dirt on her face, and the way she was leaning on the bat. "It's time to go home," he said.

Ms. Parker's coaches all hung around, watching their student stumble off to her car, waving to her as she pulled out. Then Kathy voiced the question that was in everyone's head. "Well, what do you think?" she asked.

"She learned how to stand," Ho-Pu said.

"She sort of learned how to swing," Elizabeth added.

Frank kicked at the dirt with his toe. "She can't hit worth a spit," he grumbled. "That's what matters."

"I know." Mike nodded and chewed his lip.

"And we haven't even tried her in the field," Frank went on.

Mike nodded again. "You're right," he agreed, "but, to tell the truth, she did better than I thought she would. She looks normal when she swings the bat now."

"The thing is, she *listens*," Kathy put in.

"And she keeps trying." Ho-Pu looked hard at Frank.

"I know." Frank picked up a pebble and tossed it across the field. "But it doesn't hurt to have a little natural talent."

They all laughed.

"Let's go," Mike said, before anyone had a chance to turn the mood sour again. He picked up his glove, grabbed his book bag, and headed home.

As he walked, the weight of his bag made Mike remember the books Ms. Parker had given him. His thoughts wandered to the ghostly man on the cover of *The Leatherman*. Somehow the book seemed to call to him again. Pulling it from his bag, he studied the cover and then thumbed through it, looking at the pictures. Tonight he would read, even if it meant giving up one of his shows. It surprised him to discover that the thought didn't really bother him.

6
∘∘∘
Surprises

When Mike got home, Laura was waiting on the front step with a glove, ball, and bat. "What took you so long?" she complained. "It's almost a quarter to five. I've been waiting for ages."

Mike frowned. "I never said I was coming straight home, did I?"

"No, I guess not." Laura looked uncertain. "Look, if you don't want to help me, you don't have to."

Mike resisted the urge to jump off the hook.

"Don't be dumb," he said. "I said I'd help, didn't I?"

"I know, but Daddy sort of made you." Laura twisted her hair the way she did when she was nervous.

What did she have to worry about? "Daddy didn't *make* me," he said. "I want you to look good in the game."

"Really?"

Mike poked her bat with his toe. "C'mon. Let's get started," he said. Laura jumped up and headed for the backyard.

The rear of their house bordered an open lot. Whenever it rained, the ground got wet and marshy, so the owners of the property just left it empty. Of course, when it rained, Mike couldn't use it either, but most of the time he had a great backyard ball field. Every boy and half the girls in the fourth grade envied him.

"What do you want me to do first?" Laura asked, eager now.

"Go to home plate. Show me how you stand when you're waiting for a pitch." Mike sighed heavily as he watched her walk to the piece of hard, white plastic that served as home plate. He was in no mood for this. Ms. Parker was disaster enough for any coach.

Laura arranged her bat over her right shoulder. She bent her knees and leaned forward. She looked good. "Where'd you learn to stand like that?" Mike asked, his spirits rising. "You look like you know how to play."

"I watched you." Laura winked.

"Oh." Mike was pleased. Maybe this wouldn't be so bad after all. "Let me see you swing," he said.

Laura swung.

"Get your left elbow up a little," he directed.

Laura did as she was told. Mike rubbed his hands together. Clearly, coaching his sister was going to be a whole lot easier than coaching his teacher.

"Okay. Now I'm going to try pitching to

you. Try to remember to straighten your arms as soon as you hit the ball. And then, don't stop. You have to follow through or you'll lose power."

As Mike walked across the yard, Laura tried a practice swing. He watched her straighten her arms and follow through. "Good," he called. "Now, we'll try it for real." Mike wound up and pitched.

Laura swung, connected, and sent the ball up in the air for a pop fly.

"Not bad," Mike called as he caught it. "Next time, keep the bat level. Don't scoop it."

Laura nodded.

Mike pitched. Laura swung. The ball zipped past Mike, bounced across the ground, and came to rest among the trees at the far side of the yard.

"Lookin' good, Laura," Mr. Fisher's voice called from the corner of the house. "I told you Mike would be a good teacher."

"It's not me," Mike admitted as his father came closer. "She's kind of natural at it."

"Just like her brother, huh?" Mr. Fisher grinned. "Practice with him and he'll have you hitting home runs like you were doing it forever," he called to Laura.

"I hope so," Laura said, laughing. "I really want to cream those teachers."

Teachers. Mike bumped down to earth. For a few peaceful minutes, he had forgotten about the teachers. Now he began to worry again. He didn't really care how the game turned out. He just wanted Ms. Parker and Laura to do okay. But he didn't like keeping secrets and he didn't want to be a traitor.

As it turned out, he did not have to keep his secret long. The next day, when Mike, Ms. Parker, and the other kid coaches trooped down to the field, the sixth graders were already there. Laura, out in right field, waved. Feebly, Mike waved back.

Angel, on the pitcher's mound, was shouting advice to the batter, the first baseman, and the shortstop. When he saw the fourth graders, he stopped. "We got this field," he called.

Ms. Parker stepped forward. "When will you be done?" she asked. Everyone, on and off the field, looked at her. Mike closed his eyes. He had been hoping that maybe the sixth graders wouldn't notice her. Or if they did, they might think she just happened to be around when Mike and his friends wanted to play.

Opening his eyes, Mike looked at Angel. The older boy was tossing the ball into his mitt, pulling it out, and slamming it into his mitt again. He looked angry. "We got this field until after the teacher-student game," Angel said. "We signed up for it two weeks ago."

Ms. Parker stepped back. "I didn't realize," she said. "We'll go somewhere else, then."

Angel relaxed. Apparently he didn't care what the fourth graders were up to, so long as they didn't do it where his team was practicing. He smiled at Ms. Parker, perhaps relieved that she didn't suggest sharing the field. Then, giving a little wave in Mike's direction, he turned back to the mound.

Now they were stuck. Mike stared at the occupied field. The only other place he ever played ball was his own backyard. He sure didn't want to take Ms. Parker there.

"We go to the park," Yussif said, as if he'd read Mike's thoughts. "It is near."

"They don't have a baseball field," Kathy reminded him.

"That's okay," Mike said, glad for a solution. "There are open places. We don't need an official field."

As they turned to go, a sixth grader smacked Angel's pitch far out to left field. "They play well," Ms. Parker said.

Of course they did. Mike gave her a quick look. He wondered what she'd expected.

When they got to the park, Mike pulled out

an old sock. He rolled it up and secured it with a rubber band. Then he tossed it to Kathy, who took up a pitching position about fifteen feet away.

"Why are we using a sock instead of a ball?" Ms. Parker asked.

Mike grinned. "It's better for us. We don't have to chase it all over the place. A sock doesn't go anywhere, even if you hit it hard."

"Oh." Ms. Parker looked pleased. "I'm glad you think I'm going to hit it."

"Of course you're going to hit it."

And after a while, she did. Since it was just a sock, it fell with a soft thud way short of first base, but everyone cheered as if it were a home run. Ms. Parker beamed and looked toward Mike. He lifted his hands above his head in a victory sign, and Ms. Parker beamed even more.

After she hit the sock a few times and everyone was feeling good, Mike said, "We ought to work on your fielding now." Tossing the sock aside, he stood about ten feet away and threw a ball. She caught it. Mike was so surprised, he missed when she threw it back. Everyone laughed, even Mike.

They threw the ball back and forth a few times. Her throws generally went wild, but she seemed to be able to catch. Mike felt a surge of hope. "Try tossing it up and catching it yourself," he suggested, handing her a glove. "It's a way for you to practice when we're not around."

Ms. Parker threw the ball a couple of feet into the air. It fell back in her glove. She threw it again, higher this time. It missed her glove, hitting the ground with a bounce.

"Keep your eye on the ball," Mike reminded her.

She threw it up again, this time watching it carefully.

The group stood in a circle around their teacher. As they watched the ball go up and down, they called out directions. "Bend your knees!" "Bend your arms!" "Watch the ball!"

"Don't hold your arms so high!" "Feet apart!" "Keep your eye on the ball!"

When she was catching most of the balls, even the high ones, Mike said, "I think you're ready to catch a ball someone bats out to you."

"Great!" Ms. Parker started moving toward the far end of the field.

"No, not now," Mike called to her. "We'll work on that next time."

"Are we done already?" Ms. Parker looked at her watch.

Mike nodded. "You must have eaten your vitamins this morning."

Ms. Parker threw her head back and laughed. Mike blushed. He was serious. "Just wait," Ms. Parker said, still giggling. "I may astonish us all."

When Mike got home, Laura was still not there. It was another twenty minutes before she bounced in. "How did your practice go?" he asked her.

"Great," she said. "I hit a double." She gulped a large glass of water and plopped into a kitchen chair.

"That's good. How'd you do in the field?"

"So-so. Angel says I should practice this weekend."

"Okay. Saturday morning I'll hit some out to you."

"Er . . ." Laura blushed. "You don't have to. Angel said he'd help me. He's coming over Saturday."

"Oh." Mike stared at her. He did not feel relieved and happy the way he would have expected. He felt pushed aside.

"You're not mad, are you?" Laura asked.

" 'Course not," Mike said, forcing a laugh. "I'm glad to share the work."

"Good. By the way, what's with your teacher? Was she playing ball with you guys?"

"Ms. Parker wanted to practice a little," he said lamely, "so we gave her a workout." Then, before Laura could ask any more, he

said, "I gotta go to the bathroom," and hurried out of the room.

To be on the safe side, Mike kept himself busy and out of Laura's way for the rest of the evening. He did not want to be around if the subject of the game came up. After dinner he surprised his father by taking out the garbage without being asked. Later he surprised everyone by passing up TV.

"What's the matter with Mike?" Laura asked loudly, as he walked up the stairs with his book. "This is the third time this week I've seen him read. He must be sick."

"Laura!"

Mike stopped to listen. His father's voice was angry but low. Although Mike leaned over the bannister, he couldn't make out the conversation. Still, he didn't need to hear his father's words to know that Laura was in trouble. There were benefits to reading even Ms. Parker didn't know about.

7
...
Practice, Practice, Practice

By Monday Laura was fielding balls as if she'd been playing for months. Angel had come over Saturday afternoon and spent two hours in their backyard hitting fungoes to her. He was back again on Sunday. When Mike complained about it to his parents, they looked at each other and laughed. And they wouldn't let him go into the backyard to watch. "Give her a little privacy," his father said.

"Why does she need privacy to field fungoes?"

Mike's father leaned close to him, as if he were going to tell a secret. "Angel's a boy," he said.

Well, of course Angel was a boy. Mike stared at his father. "You mean he *likes* her?" he asked, finally catching on.

"I think so." Mr. Fisher nodded. Suddenly Mike understood a lot of things. He felt better, too, about having been fired as Laura's coach.

He was still Ms. Parker's coach, however. *Her* game, unfortunately, did *not* improve over the weekend. If Ms. Parker was going to astonish them, Mike thought, she'd better get busy. So far the only astonishing thing about her game was that it was still so bad. When Yussif and Ho-Pu took turns hitting balls to her, the only ones she could catch were those that came right to her. When she had to move to the ball, she couldn't seem to get into position.

"Get it when it's in front of you," Frank

said, as she grabbed helplessly for a ball that bounced between her legs.

The next time, the ball shot past her.

"Don't reach toward the side," Elizabeth advised. "You want to block it with your body."

Ms. Parker nodded, ready to block, but this time the ball went over her head.

"Try again," Mike urged. Ms. Parker tried. And tried. And tried. The ball always seemed to be where Ms. Parker was not.

And then, when Mike was wondering if there was *anything* he could say that would help, she was in the right place at the right time, and a ball landed smack in the middle of her glove. Ms. Parker got so excited she hugged Frank, who turned beet red. Then she signaled Yussif to bat another ball her way.

On Tuesday they began serious work on throwing. "Hold the ball with your fingers," Mike explained, "and bring your arm way back. As you throw, step forward."

Ms. Parker looked down at her feet.

"Don't watch your feet," Mike said patiently. "You have to look where you're throwing."

After several tries, Ms. Parker did it right. She stepped forward as she threw, kept her eye on the target, and let go at the right moment.

"Now all you need is practice," Mike said.

Ms. Parker practiced all afternoon. By the end of the day, she got the ball all the way to first base.

"Amazing!" Frank said.

"She worked for it," Kathy reminded him.

And Ms. Parker kept working. On Wednesday she practiced batting and catching and throwing. On Thursday she practiced catching and throwing and batting. On Friday she practiced some more.

Monday afternoon, twenty-two hours before the big game, the teachers had a practice session. "Let's watch," Mike said. "Maybe we'll get some last minute ideas for her." Ms. Parker's coaches climbed the hill overlooking the ball field. The sixth graders were already there. "Checking out the opposition," Angel explained, as if anyone didn't know.

Mike scrunched down on the far side of a tree, many yards from where the older kids were sitting. His sister found him immediately. "What's going on?" she asked.

"The teachers are going to practice."

"C'mon Mike. That's not what I mean." Laura slid down next to him. "Everyone knows you've been helping Ms. Parker."

Mike dropped his eyes.

"How could you do that?" Laura demanded. "I mean, you knew I was playing."

Mike took a deep breath. "It has nothing to do with you. I wasn't trying to mess up your game."

"What then?"

"It was just to help Ms. Parker. She couldn't play. I mean, at all. Zip. Zero. She was going to look really stupid."

"So you taught her?"

"As much as we could in two weeks. She's still no Cal Ripkin."

"You helped *me*, too."

"Yeah." Did Laura think he'd double-crossed her? She sure looked peculiar. "Are you mad?" he asked.

Laura picked an imaginary thread off his shirt and shook her head. "You're okay," she said as she started back to Angel and the other sixth graders. "I just hope you didn't teach her *too* much."

It was not much of a practice. Mr. Plumber, the principal, tossed soft, underhand pitches, as one by one, the teachers came to bat. Mr. Kloski really clobbered the ball, and Ms. Stone and Ms. Finkle each hit respectable drives. Mike was relieved when Mrs. Russo needed six or seven chances before she managed a little hit; it made Ms. Parker look okay. It only took *her* four tries.

"She'd have been out in a game," Frank muttered.

Ms. Parker was nervous, Mike could tell. Would she fall apart under pressure? He watched uneasily as she ran out to take a turn on first base. Throughout the batting exercise, the teachers kept shifting around, taking turns as catcher and fielders. Ms. Parker missed the first ball that came her way, but caught the second. Nothing was hit to right field when she held that position.

After a few rounds of batting and fielding, Mr. Plumber announced that the practice was over. The whole thing had taken less than twenty minutes.

"We didn't learn much from that," Elizabeth complained.

"I don't know." Ho-Pu shook his head. "Ms. Parker did hit the ball, and she doesn't look much worse than the others."

"Anybody could've hit those marshmallows," Frank groused. "She'll have to handle much tougher stuff tomorrow—and she won't get four tries, either."

"Then she'll do it in three," Kathy snapped.

Mike put up his hand. "Relax, guys. Now who are we gonna cheer for?"

When Mike got home that afternoon, his mother was in front of the house, digging in a bare patch of dirt. "Aren't you working today?" Mike asked.

Leaning back on her heels, Mrs. Fisher smiled at him and shook her head. "They had to do something with the electrical system," she explained. "The computers were down, and the lights were off, so they sent us home early."

"Why doesn't the electricity ever go off in school?" Mike complained.

His mother laughed. "You'd just have to sit

near the window. They wouldn't send you home." She picked up one of the small pots of ivy that sat on the front step.

"Will those little shoots fill up that big spot?" Mike asked.

"Give them time," his mother said. "Ivy spreads fast." She looked up at him and noticed the book in his hand. "What are you reading?" she asked.

Mike turned his wrist, showing her the cover.

"*The Chocolate Touch*," she read aloud. "Is it good?"

Mike nodded. "It's about this kid who turns everything he touches into chocolate. It's funny."

"I'm glad. I like to see you reading."

"So does Ms. Parker," Mike admitted.

His mother laughed. "I expect she does. Teachers don't devote every spare second of the day to baseball, you know."

You haven't met Ms. Parker, Mike thought

with a grin. Stepping over the ivy, he opened the door and slid *The Chocolate Touch* onto the hall table. He felt pleased. His reading was going well these days. He'd finished *The Leatherman*, and Ms. Parker had liked what he said in his journal. She'd written *very good* where he said that the reason for Ben's dream was to get the reader into a creepy mood. And where he wrote that he thought the author wanted us to be nice to people even when they are odd, she had written, *I agree.* Later, she'd stopped him to tell him how much she had enjoyed his comments. "It was so perceptive of you to see that saying Ben's name was like giving him a present," she'd said. "I hadn't thought of it quite that way before, but I think you are absolutely right."

Mike decided he liked writing about the books he read. After he'd told Ms. Parker that he thought the fat sports book she'd found for him was boring, she told him to write all the things he didn't like about it in his journal.

"Sometimes it's fun to write a bad review," she said with a wink. And when Mike asked if he had to finish reading the book, she was shocked. "Of course not!" she said. "There are too many wonderful books available to waste time with bad ones." How sensible, Mike thought.

As he thought about his books and his journal, Mike realized that he'd stopped worrying about Ms. Parker. That was another good thing about reading. He went back to the hall table and picked up *The Chocolate Touch*. If chocolate couldn't get Ms. Parker off his mind, nothing could.

8

The Game

In Ms. Parker's class, they were supposed to read after lunch. Mike held a book in his hands, but his eyes followed Ms. Parker as she moved around the room, picking up papers and folders and putting them down someplace else. Finally, he slid out of his seat and walked up to her. "How are you doing?" he asked.

She shrugged. "I guess I'm as ready as I'll ever be."

That was certainly true. Mike hoped she

was ready enough. Never had he seen anyone work so hard. She was five hundred percent better. If she didn't lose her nerve, with a little luck she'd be fine.

Luck. Mike remembered his glove. He thought about how it cradled the Mickey Mantle ball every night. He still didn't believe in magic, but he figured Ms. Parker could use all the help she could get. Impulsively, he went to his desk and pulled out his mitt. He brought it back and shoved it into her hand. "Use my glove today," he said. "It's been good to me. Maybe it will bring you luck."

Ms. Parker took Mike's glove, her face solemn as she thanked him.

Mike wanted to tell her to be careful with it. He thought about all the nights he oiled it and curled it around the ball. Yet, it just didn't seem right to tell a teacher to be careful. He looked at his glove uneasily. His own hand felt very naked.

"I'll take good care of your glove, Mike,"

Ms. Parker assured him. "You don't have to worry about it."

"I wasn't worried," he said.

At 1:45 the fourth grade room-mothers arrived and took the class outside, freeing Ms. Parker to mill about the baseball diamond with her teammates. As the classes found places on the hill, Mr. Plumber moved from group to group to help the parent volunteers keep the crowd controlled. Spirits were high. The younger children waved banners to cheer on their teachers. The older kids waved banners too, mostly supporting the sixth grade. To add to the general confusion, several mothers with toddlers and a couple with infants in strollers collected in a noisy, unruly group near Mike's class. Here and there, a father arrived.

Angel moved among the sixth graders, giving out last minute instructions. Mike swallowed hard as he watched him stop to talk to one and then another of the older kids. They were so big and they played so well. He wondered what would happen to Ms. Parker when Angel pitched to her. Laura, he noticed, stood off by herself, twisting her hair. It made him worry about her, too.

The sixth grade was up first. The teachers spread out, taking their places in the field. Ms. Parker ran out to right field. "There's not much action there," Mike had advised her. "Mostly it's only lefties who hit to the right." Grateful for the tip, Ms. Parker had asked for and gotten that low-key position.

The first sixth grader hit a line drive past third base for a base hit. The second hit a grounder, moving the first runner along. When it was Laura's turn, she hit the ball with a nice, solid thwack. As she ran, Mike could hear Angel making lots of noise cheering for her. She landed triumphantly safe on first. Good. Mike could relax about her.

Out in the field, Ms. Parker did things like punch her fist into Mike's glove, but no balls came her way. After a while, the inning was over. The sixth grade had two runs.

Since she was at the bottom of a lackluster batting order, Ms. Parker was not up until the end of the second inning. Even so, Mike never took his eyes off her. She gnawed at a fingernail all through the first inning, and Mike had to shove his hands in his pockets so he wouldn't chew his own. Finally, it was her turn.

Angel's pitch came in fast, right across the plate. Ms. Parker tipped the ball to the shortstop, who easily threw her out at first base.

"She hit it," Ho-Pu told Mike. "Next time she'll get on base." But she didn't. Her next time up at bat, she hit a grounder to the pitcher, resulting in a double play and the end of the fourth inning.

"At least she's connecting," Frank said anxiously.

But she began to have trouble in the field, too. She fumbled a ball hit by Lefty Jones, getting it to first base too late for the out. Another throw went wide, saved only by the quick reflexes of the kindergarten teacher. "Never mind," Elizabeth reassured Mike. "She caught the balls and got them to the right base. It's more than she could have done two weeks ago." It was true, but Mike was hoping for something better—like with Laura. His sister had gotten another single in the fifth inning and tagged Ms. Finkle out at second in the top of the sixth. Mike wanted Ms. Parker to come away from the game with something memorable, too.

By the time his teacher came to bat in the ninth, the sixth grade was leading four to nothing. There was one out—by Mr. Kloski, who had popped out four times so far—and nobody on base. The first pitch was wide, and Ms. Parker let it go. "Way to go!" Yussif yelled when the umpire called, "Ball!"

The second pitch was low. "Maybe they'll walk her," Kathy muttered.

"No." Frank shook his head. "Here comes a good one."

Ms. Parker swung, and everyone leapt to their feet as the ball drove past the shortstop. Ms. Parker was safe on first. Her coaches cheered. As Mike moved forward to get a better view, he realized he'd been forgetting to breathe. He let out an ear-splitting whoop.

Mrs. Stanley, a third grade teacher who never wore anything but elegant clothes and high heels, came up next. Although she'd gotten on base once in last year's game, so far today she'd struck out twice and hit a little grounder to the pitcher. The outfielders, expecting no more than a dribble, moved in closer. To everyone's amazement, Mrs. Stanley hit a long, high drive to center field. The center fielder, out of position, desperately ran back, but the ball sailed over his head.

"Third, third," the fourth graders screamed. Ms. Parker followed orders. Once safe on third, she waved to her students, who waved back wildly. Mike's heart was pounding as fast as if he'd just run around the field twice.

The teachers were excited now too, and yelled, "C'mon, Sally," and "Give us a hit," as Sally Stone, the young and athletic fifth grade teacher, took her place at bat. The outfielders hitched up their pants and pounded their gloves. Angel wound up and threw a hard, fast pitch.

When Ms. Stone hit a hard grounder into left field, Ms. Parker started running.

"HOME! HOME! HOME!" Mike shouted. He could hear Yussif and Frank and Kathy yelling, too.

"HOME!" yelled Mr. Plumber, the principal.

"HOME!" yelled the other teachers.

Ms. Parker crossed home plate. Everyone cheered, but the fourth grade coaches cheered loudest of all and ran down the hill to congratulate her. Ms. Parker hugged Mike. In fact, Ms. Parker hugged everybody. This time Frank didn't blush. He even hugged her back.

By the time they all had finished hugging, the game was over. The sixth grade had won, four to one, but Mike didn't care. The teachers' one run was Ms. Parker's.

"You were great," Mike told her as she handed him his glove.

"Not me, Mike, *you*. You're a wonderful teacher. I'd never have been able to hit that ball if you hadn't helped me."

Mike was glad to have evened the score a little. She had certainly helped him enough, finding him books instead of yelling when he hadn't done his journal. Not many teachers would have been so patient. He studied the adults who were still hanging around home plate. "I was wondering something," he said.

"What's that?" Ms. Parker put a hand on his shoulder and started them in the direction of their classroom.

"I was wondering how the other teachers feel about this game." The images of Mr.

Kloski hitting into his fourth out and Mrs. Russo swinging her bat and missing every time were suddenly very vivid.

"That's interesting that you should ask that, Mike." Ms. Parker stopped walking. "We were just talking about it this morning in the teacher's lounge. You know, most of us are not very good at baseball."

"It's fun for the kids," he said quickly.

Ms. Parker nodded. "Sure. That's why we play. But we were thinking of doing something else as well, maybe in the fall."

"You mean like a basketball game?"

"Yes." Ms. Parker nodded. "Except, what we were actually thinking about was volley-ball."

"Volleyball! But we hardly ever play volleyball, except once in a while in gym. I'm no good at it."

Ms. Parker looked at him and winked. "But I'm *very* good at it," she said.